The Queen & Mr Brown
Meet the Rats

James Francis Wilkins

Published by the Natural History Museum, London

For my friends the rats

Once again many thanks to
Steve Woods and Colin Ziegler
for their advice and support
...and patience

First published by the Natural History Museum
Cromwell Road, London SW7 5BD
© Natural History Museum, London, 2017
Text and illustrations © James Francis Wilkins

Hardback ISBN 978 0 565 09438 6
Paperback ISBN 978 0 565 09446 1

A catalogue record for this book is available from the
British Library.

Reproduction by Saxon Digital Services
Printed in China by 1010 Printing International Limited

'Come on Mr Brown, we're late!' Mr Brown was frantically gobbling biscuits. He always did before they left the Palace. He was never sure when he would get another meal.

The Queen was excited because the animals that live in London's Natural History Museum had invited them to go on a mystery tour.

They had arranged to meet in Cromwell Road in front of the Museum, but when they arrived there was no-one there. They were beginning to think they were in the wrong place when something strange happened.

The pavement next to them opened up and the
polar bear and toucan rose slowly from beneath.
'How very extraordinary!' said the Queen.

'Come on, climb aboard!' said the bear, 'We're ready
to go!' So aboard they climbed and sank slowly down,
with the pavement closing up again over their heads.

They emerged into a dark tunnel and the toucan
flew ahead, shrieking 'Follow me!' He landed in
front of a large black door.

The polar bear tapped a code into the control panel
to the left of the door and the door slid slowly open.

'Goodness gracious!' said the Queen. 'Jumping jellyfish!'
thought Mr Brown. There were rows of animals working
on computers in front of what looked like a giant conker.

It was Conkerdor, the space transporter that can take you anywhere in the animal kingdom. 'Welcome to Mission Control!' said the bear. 'Let me explain how it works.'

'The Conkerdor has a computer which decides where to take you and gives you information about the animals you will meet. The toucan will help you. Good luck and have fun!'

'A computer?' thought Mr Brown. 'I'm not
sure I want to be looked after by a computer!'
The Queen on the other hand loved trying out
anything new.

Without hesitation she climbed up the steps into Conkerdor.
'Isn't it exciting Mr Brown! I can't wait to find out where
we're going!' Reluctantly, Mr Brown climbed up after her.
He was her best friend and he couldn't desert her now.

They strapped themselves in and the toucan asked Conkerdor where they were going. 'Today we will visit a family of rats. Here are some interesting facts about rats.' it replied.

'Oh no!' thought Mr Brown, 'I knew this was a bad idea!'

'Did it say rats?' enquired the Queen, slightly taken aback. 'Yes Ma'am it did.' said the toucan, chuckling to himself. 'How fascinating...I know nothing about rats!' replied the Queen. Mr Brown, on the other hand, was far from convinced.

Rats are shy
and clever.

Rats can swim through
sewers and come out of
toilets.

Rats can spread disease
because of their fleas.

Rats are studied by
scientists because they
are like humans.

Rats can go through
tiny holes because
their bones fold up.

Rats travel around
the world on ships.

Rats can eat
almost everything.

Rats will probably
be here long after
humans are gone.

The roof opened and sunlight flooded in. 'You may unfasten your seatbelts. We have arrived!' announced the Conkerdor.

The Queen and Mr Brown cautiously peered out. They were greeted by squeals of delight. 'Hello my friend,' the toucan called down. ' I haven't seen you for ages. What have you been up to all this time?'

A big, fat rat was looking up at them. He was surrounded by young rats. 'Oh, nothing special,' he replied, 'just another eight kids. You know how it is!'

The Queen and Mr Brown walked down the steps and were immediately surrounded by young rats. They seemed friendly but they still made Mr Brown feel nervous.

The Queen puckered her nose. 'What a strange smell!'
she said. 'Are we...in a rubbish dump?' 'Yes of course'
said the rat. 'Come on, I'll show you!'

'Isn't it a glorious view!' Stretched out below them was
nothing but garbage as far as the eye could see. 'I used to live
in the country' continued the rat, ' and life was so hard...

but here I have everything I want! Paradise!
Sometimes I come here in the evening to watch
the sun set and think what a lucky rat I am!'

The rat took them to his home and was just introducing them to his large family when some of them began to sniff the air. 'Dinner is served!' one cried and they all scampered outside.

A rubbish truck was approaching down the rough track. Seagulls circled in the sky. All waited patiently until it had dumped its load.

Then they all dashed out to grab the tastiest morsels.
The seagulls were trying to snatch them too because
they were also hungry, but the rats were quicker...

...and they returned home with lots of rotten,
stinking food which they dumped in a heap.
Then, without further ceremony,...

...they began to eat. The big, fat rat had
a feeling his guests would not enjoy the
feast so he sent some of his kids to the

supermarket to buy a packet of
gingersnaps. The toucan had told him
that this was their favourite food.

After the rats had eaten they fell asleep and began to snore. By this time the Queen and Mr Brown were also worn out and they too fell asleep.

They slept until a young rat poked his father in the belly. 'Are you coming Daddy?' he shrieked. 'Oooooh!' groaned his father. 'You're ready are you? Alright, we'll be along in a minute.' He then roused the others and they all trooped outside.

He explained to his guests that his kids had created a little show especially for them. He led them to an open-air theatre...

...and took them to a large wooden box in the front row. 'The Royal Box!' he said grandly. They took their seats and the show began.

And what a show it was! The rats danced around
the stage to music coming from a broken radio. For
lighting there was a string of Christmas tree lights.

They were so agile, their movements so precise
and the choreography so wonderful! The audience
could not have enough of their acrobatics.

They sprang sideways over one another, built rat pyramids, ran along tightropes, jumped through hoops. It was such a spectacular show that the Queen and Mr Brown...

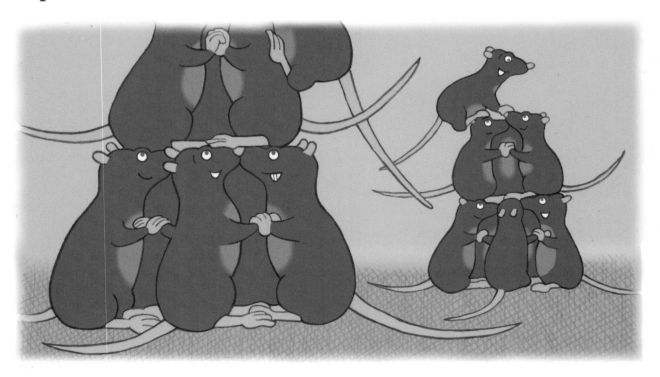

...completely forgot that they were in a rubbish dump and they even forgot the stink. As a grand finale the young rats did the Rat Rave.

We are rats

We're quicker than cats

And we're twice as clever

    Don't need shoes

    Don't need socks

    Don't need soap

    Don't need clocks

    Don't need rules

    Don't need schools

        We can writhe

        We can wriggle

        We can laugh

        We can giggle

        We can squeak

        We can squeal

            We can fart

            We can burp

            We can slobber

            We can slurp

                We can poo

                We can pee

                We can dribble in the sea

                    We are rats

                    We are alive

                    We will survive

The Queen's eyes grew larger and larger and she felt herself blushing. As the applause faded she said quietly, choosing her words with care, 'Your children are quite unforgettable.'

The big, fat rat beamed with pleasure.

'Yes they're a good bunch aren't they!

I'm so proud of them!'

The toucan said it was time to leave so
they walked back together to Conkerdor
where they said their goodbyes. This took a
considerable amount of time because all of the
rats insisted on shaking the Queen's hand.

Then the Queen and Mr Brown climbed back into
Conkerdor and gave one last wave. The hatch closed
and before they knew it they were back in the Museum.

The polar bear was there to greet them and escorted them
back onto the streets of London via the secret entrance.

'Well Mr Brown, what did you think about that? Aren't rats astonishing…and they eat all our waste! But I wouldn't change our life for theirs in a million years. I am so glad we have our Palace to come home to!' Mr Brown agreed fervently. For the first time in his life he realised that he was a very spoilt dog.

The Queen was completely exhausted, but delighted with how their first mystery tour had gone. As she snuggled into bed she called down to Mr Brown, 'Do you know what Mr Brown? I've just realised there is no more beautiful smell in the world than that of fresh clean sheets!'

Mr Brown was also happy to be in his bed...

he was already fast asleep.